MCXI: Confessions

A Collection of Erotic Stories
Inspired by True Events

by Eda Boss

First Edition
Published by Eda Boss Publishing
ISBN: 979-8-218-73833-4

Cover and interior design by Eda Boss
Printed in the United States of America

Content & Safety Disclaimer

This book contains fictional stories with explicit sexual content intended for mature audiences only. It explores themes of power dynamics, seduction, emotional tension, and consensual adult relationships.

The content in this book is not intended to serve as medical, psychological, or relationship advice. Any scenarios or behaviors described should not be interpreted as guidance or instruction. Always prioritize communication, safety, and informed consent in real life.

The author and publisher are not liable for any outcomes resulting from attempts to imitate or act on the content within these stories. Please consult licensed professionals for any physical, emotional, or mental health concerns.

Table of Contents

Pretty Girl

Inspired by the MCXI Candle — Pretty Girl (Pink sugar crystal)

They were both popular. Both hot.

Both followed each other online for years—liking stories, sharing memes, reacting to thirst traps.

Mutual friends.

Mutual thirst.

But they never linked.

She finally DMed him first.

He thought it was a setup, maybe she was trying to make her ex jealous.

But she'd been crushing on him since forever.

She just finally said something.

Their first night hanging out was supposed to be chill. Drinks. Vibes. Maybe a kiss.

But she wanted to straddle him in the backseat before they even made it inside.

And once through the door, she was already undoing his belt.

He was stunned.

"You're a pretty girl… I didn't expect you to be this—."

"Nasty?" she smirked, dropping to her knees.

She did everything.

And he meant everything.

The kind of sex that made you question if this was real life or some alternate dimension where beautiful women were also porn stars.

She licked places. Said things.

Climbed on top and rode him backwards while sucking his toes.

At one point, she told him to spit in her mouth.

He did it.

They fucked so long and hard, neither of them remembered when they finally passed out—just that they woke up tangled in each other, sore and smiling.

The next morning, she wore his hoodie and made him pancakes—naked.

He looked at her like he'd just seen a majestic being... a unicorn.

"You're wild," he whispered.

She winked. "I know."

That afternoon, she whispered a fantasy to him.

She wanted to play helpless. Tied. Taken. Controlled.

She described it in detail:

2

Home alone. Washing her hair.

Steam rising. Music playing. Vulnerable.

Then, he walks in.

Silent. Masked. Rope in hand.

"I want to pretend I don't see you," she said, eyes already dark with desire. "You just grab me. Bend me over. Tie me up. Take me like I'm yours."

He hesitated for a second. That level of kink was new to him.

But the way she bit her bottom lip as she spoke—the flush on her chest, the wetness gathering between her thighs—he couldn't say no.

She left a key under the doormat the next evening.

He parked a block away. Wore all black. Pulled the mask over his face just before stepping onto her porch.

His hands were shaking—but not from nerves. From anticipation.

He slipped inside. The music was playing low.

The bathroom light was on. Steam poured from the cracked door.

She was in the shower, back turned, rinsing her hair like nothing was happening. Just as she'd described.

He stood there watching for a moment—then moved in silence.

3

She gasped when she felt him behind her, a gloved hand covering her mouth, the other yanking her towel off the hook.

He pressed her wet body against the counter and wrapped the rope around her wrists like he'd practiced.

Tight. But gentle. Controlled. But possessive.

She didn't say a word. Just exhaled a breathy moan and arched her back as he bent her over the sink, spreading her legs.

He slid inside slowly—deliberately. She was already soaked.

The mask stayed on.

The only sound was skin slapping skin, and her whimper echoing against the tile.

He grabbed her hair. Bit her shoulder. Spit in her mouth when she begged for it.

By the time she came, she was trembling legs shaking, arms bound, eyes glassy with pleasure.

When it was over, he untied her wrists, kissed her neck, and whispered,

"You owe me pecan waffles in the morning."

She smiled, laughing, and said,

"You can have any fucking waffles your heart desires."

Goddess

Inspired by the MCXI Candle — Goddess (Pineapple and sage)

She moved through the world like a soft breeze scented with sage and citrus.

Long crocheted locs kissed her waist. Waist beads shimmered under her crop tops like hidden secrets. She always smelled like mango butter and moonlight.

Her garden was her altar—rows of mint, basil, and tomatoes growing beside lavender and lemongrass.

Crystals lined her windowsills.

Her playlists floated from Jill Scott to Sade, Erykah Badu to Glorilla—because duality was divine.

She was Goddess. And she knew it.

Every Sunday, she walked the farmer's market barefoot in sandals that barely held on, sipping hibiscus tea and letting the energy guide her.

That's when she saw him.

He stood behind a small table stacked with square-shaped jars—massage oil candles with labels scribbled in calligraphy.

His smile was grounded, his aura clean. But it was the tattoo on his left arm that held her: the face of a celestial woman crowned with planets, watching over the Earth.

"Beautiful," she said softly.

He looked up from arranging the display. "Thanks. I've been working on this setup for a while."

She leaned in slightly; eyes fixed on his arm. "I was talking about the tattoo."

He smiled. "Women are God's greatest creation."

She grinned. "It actually kind of looks like me."

He glanced at his arm, then back at her. "You know, you're right."

She reached for one of the candles and brought it to her nose. Sage and pineapple.

"And this?"

"That's my best-seller. I call it Goddess."

She smiled slowly. "Seems accurate."

She purchased the Goddess candle and took his business card off the table. As she stood there, she texted him her number.

"I like your energy," she said softly. "It's something powerful."

The next day, at exactly 11:11 AM, she texted him:

"I'd like to see you…"

He replied within moments.

"Name the time and place."

She dropped a pin.

6

"My garden. Sunset."

Her front yard was modest, but the backyard was her sanctuary. A place of symmetry and wild beauty—blossoming flowers next to collard greens, towering sunflowers beside peppermint shrubs.

It smelled like rainwater and rebirth.

He followed the scent of sage through the open gate.

She was barefoot on the grass, wearing a flowing rust-colored dress and golden bangles that jingled like wind chimes. Her locs were tied up, exposing her glowing shoulders.

A quilted blanket was spread across the manicured lawn, with dishes carefully placed, steamed lentils, roasted eggplant, herbed couscous, and fresh-squeezed watermelon juice in glass bottles.

"You cooked all this?" he asked, already smiling.

"From scratch," she said, handing him a plate. "Even the juice."

They sat. They ate. They laughed until their cheeks hurt.

He complimented the seasoning—she replied that she cooks like she loves: slow, layered, with intention.

He said her energy was delicious.

She said, "Wait until dessert."

As the sun dipped low, she reached across the blanket, brushing her fingers over the planets inked on his arm.

"I wasn't joking," she whispered. "I wanted to see you. But what I really want—is to feel you."

He set his glass down. She stood and offered her hand.

"Come," she said.

He followed her through the garden gate, along a stone path that led to a small, candlelit room detached from the house.

Bamboo wind chimes swayed gently overhead, and an MCXI Goddess candle flickered from a corner altar.

The same sage and pineapple scent greeted him—soft and sultry.

Inside, she stripped down slowly—first the bangles, then the dress—revealing only her waist beads and a look of absolute calm.

He undressed too. No words, just breath.

She guided him to a wide rattan mat surrounded by pillows, then lowered herself into his lap, wrapping her arms around his neck.

When she slid down onto him, it felt like a spell had been cast.

She was soft, dripping, already pulsing around him.

Her hips moved in slow, intentional circles, like she was invoking something sacred.

Their bodies rocked in time with the wind.

She whispered into his ear—not dirty talk, but declarations of desire:

8

"You taste like peace… your energy is rich… I want you in my spirit."

He was captivated. She was riding him like a ritual, her breasts brushing his chest, her moans rolling off her tongue like sacred chants.

His hands traced her thighs, her back, her waist beads clicking faintly with each grind.

When she clenched around him, he could feel the tremble—like a storm building.

Her climax came like thunder in slow motion. Her legs shook. Her back arched. A tear slid down her cheek.

He held her.

Then he flipped her over, gently, reverently.

Her body curved beneath him like a crescent moon as he thrust into her again—slow, deep, divine.

She gripped the pillow above her head, gasping as he whispered:

"This isn't just sex… this is alchemy."

When he came, it was with a guttural groan, buried in her neck, his arms wrapped tight around her belly like he was holding onto the Earth itself.

Later, she curled into him, fingertips tracing the solar system on his forearm.

"I manifested you," she said sleepily.

He kissed her forehead.

"I've been orbiting you my whole life."

And in the dim room, beside the flickering candle, the Goddess melted slowly—as did she.

Lover

Inspired by the MCXI Candle — Lover (Chocolate & Roses).

He'd been on the road for four days. Two conventions. Two airport delays.

And all he wanted was her.

Not a drink. Not sleep.

Her.

When he opened the front door, the scent hit him—chocolate and roses.

The lights were dim.

His wife stood in the center of the living room in red lace, holding a glass of wine, eyes locked on him.

"Welcome home," she whispered. "I missed you."

She walked over slowly and fed him a strawberry dipped in chocolate.

Then she kissed the wine off his lips and pressed her body into his.

They didn't make it to the bedroom right away.

She unbuckled his belt as he kissed down her neck, his hands sliding beneath the lace.

"I want you to taste what you've been missing," she breathed.

Later, upstairs…

Her body arched as he licked chocolate from her inner thigh.

She giggled, moaned, then grabbed his face.

"I need you inside me. Now."

He flipped her onto all fours, kissed the small of her back, then entered her slowly from behind.

"God, I missed this dick," she said through gasps.

He gripped her hips and gave her what she craved— deep strokes that had her moaning into the mattress.

And when he finally pulled out, he released all over her ass—like he was painting a masterpiece, and pleasure was the paint.

She laughed breathlessly. "Next time… when you leave, the dick stays home with me."

El Jefe

Inspired by the MCXI Candle – El Jefe (Spiced Honey, Tonka, and Cigar).

Everyone called him Boss.

Not because he asked for it-because it fit.

Ex-Army.

Successful entrepreneur.

Fitness carved into every inch of his frame like a living sculpture.

He didn't lead with bravado. He led with energy.

You felt him before you saw him.

He didn't chase women. He didn't need to.

Their smiles softened. Their posture shifted. Their hands itched to serve-just to be close.

Knowing he could have them was more satisfying than the chase.

He only smoked cigars in private, or at his members-only lounge- a dim, luxurious place where off-the-record deals moved industries and egos bowed quietly.

No selfies. No noise. Just unspoken influence.

She hadn't expected to see him that night.

She came for a business drink, following a colleague's invitation to discuss branding over bourbon.

But the moment she stepped inside the velvet-curtained lounge, her eyes locked onto the man seated near the corner.

Fitted charcoal suit. Bald head, clean and commanding.

Tattooed forearms crossed. Beard trimmed.

A soft flame flickered beside him-a MCXI El Jefe candle casting a scent of spiced honey, tonka, and cigar into the air.

She hesitated for a moment, then approached. "Hi," she smiled. "I remember you.. from the gym." He looked up, calm and confident.

"Yes. I remember you too."

She leaned in a bit closer, voice low and smooth.

"Make sure we talk before you leave."

She paused, then added with a playful smirk:

"You better.. or I'll trip you next time you walk past me at the gym."

She laughed, walking back to her table, hips swaying.

He watched her go-expression unreadable.

True to her demand, just before leaving, he walked over to her table.

They chatted briefly-minimal small talk. Her curiosity got the best of her.

"Tell me something about you," she said. "What do you like? Any fantasies? What makes your blood flow?"

He stared at her a beat too long. Then he answered, calm and clear:

"Witnessing self-gratification." Her lips parted.

"You mean.. watching?"

"Mmm," he nodded. "But not just the act. The build-up. The denial. The surrender."

She shifted in her seat. Her pulse quickened.

They exchanged numbers. Eye contact lingered longer than it should've.

That night, she couldn't sleep.

His presence haunted her.

His voice echoed like bass through silk sheets.

The next evening, she texted him:

"What are you doing tonight?" "Waiting for you," he replied.

She arrived at his place just after nine.

Everything about the space was intentional-dark wood floors, warm lights, minimalist furniture, jazz humming low in the background.

A single El Jefe candle burned by the window. The air was thick with its masculine scent.

When he opened the door, she stepped into him-arms around his neck.

He hugged her, arms firm around her waist.

She inhaled slowly, like she was trying to make his air touch her soul.

No small talk. No hesitations.

She walked past him, found the velvet chaise, and slowly spread her thighs-fingers sliding over bare skin.

"Edge yourself," he said. "Then stop." Her breath stuttered.

"Don't come until I tell you."

She obeyed. Barely.

Her moans filled the room, needy and soft.

"Do you want your release?"

She nodded, on the verge of begging.

"Then earn it."

She crawled to him like she'd done it before.

He stood, gripped her locs, and fed her every inch. "Ask me," he commanded.

"Please," she gasped, mouth full. "Let me come."

Just as he groaned and began to throb in her mouth, he gave it:

"Come now."

16

She squirted uncontrollably, her body trembling as her orgasm splashed the hardwood floor.

He released into her mouth-deep and slow-his grip firm on her head as she took all of him.

Later, draped over his lap like silk, she whispered, dazed.

"You didn't even touch me, and I feel fucked." He chuckled, stroking her back.

" Just make sure you clean my floor before you go."
"Your DNA is all over the place."

They both laugh.

Dommé

Inspired by the MCXI Candle — Dommé (Red Ginger and Saffron).

She spotted him in the rope aisle at Home Depot.

Of all places.

The colors caught her eye first — neon lime, black nylon, crimson red — before she noticed his cart.

Duct tape. Smooth pine planks. Carabiners. Suspicious. Deliciously suspicious.

Mistress J didn't believe in coincidence. Only instinct.

As she picked up a coil of rope, she turned slightly — just enough to see him peek into her cart: zip ties, nitrile gloves.

He was good. Didn't flinch.

"I love a man who knows his way around a toolbox," she said casually.

He looked up, smiling. "I actually have a pretty impressive toolbox. Lately I've found myself indulging in some DIY projects."

She smirked. "Maybe I should get your contact info. One of us is bound to need.. assistance."

He pulled out his phone without hesitation.

"So, what's your name?" "J," she replied.

"J?"

"Yes, just J."

"Okay, Just J."

He took her number and slid his phone back into his pocket as she turned and walked away.

"Lewis," he called after her.

She paused, glancing over her shoulder.

"That's my name. In case you need more than a number."

She smiled. "I always do."

That night, her phone lit up.

Lewis:

Just checking in..

Wanted to make sure the rope and tape made it home safe.

J:

Ever heard of The Velvet Rope?

Lewis:

Once or twice.

Stop by Friday night. I'll make sure you're on the list.

Friday Night. The Velvet Rope.

A sanctuary for Dominants, submissives, switches, and voyeurs alike.

The bass pulsed like a heartbeat. Red haze and dark corners.

And there she was.

Mistress J stood on a raised platform. Leather corset. Thigh-high boots. Masked. Commanding.

A woman — bound to a Saint Andrew's Cross in familiar neon lime green rope — writhed under her touch.

Mistress J moved like silk over steel. Her voice sliced through the low hum of moans and music.

The crowd was enchanted. Some in suits and elegant dresses. Some in latex. Some in nothing but chains. All watching.

Lewis froze. He'd seen her before. Many times. But now, he knew. The energy was unmistakable.

After the scene, she vanished.

Then his phone lit up.

Room Three. Now.

He entered the private room. The scent of leather, red ginger, and saffron filled the air. Candles flickered.

She stood at the center, mask still on, arms crossed, eyes gleaming.

"You bring your toys?" She asked.

He opened his bag — a wand vibrator, heavy leather floggers, nipple clamps, and a square glass jar of MCXI El Jefe — spiced honey, tonka, and cigar.

She stepped forward. "Let's see what that toolbox of yours can really do." Before he could answer, the door creaked open.

A striking, dark-skinned woman stepped in — lean and toned, like a track star. She hesitated when she saw them.

J curled a finger. "Come."

"Yes, Mistress," she said, stepping forward.

"Isn't he sexy?" J asked.

"Yes, Mistress."

"Would you like to play with him?"

"Yes, Mistress."

Lewis spoke. "What's your name?"

"Mahogany, Sir."

"Well, Mahogany," he said, "you'll be my assistant tonight." J's breath hitched.

Lewis approached her with deliberate confidence. "Strip," he said, voice like heat.

She obeyed.

He tied her to the Saint Andrew's Cross — firm, skilled, patient.

He lit the El Jefe candle. The scent of cigar and warm honey filled the room.

He let hot wax drip down her thighs, her nipples, the inside of her arms. She gasped with each touch.

He rubbed the wand slowly against her clit — not quite pressing — edging her until her legs trembled.

He turned to Mahogany. "You enjoying the show?"

"Yes, Sir," she whispered.

"You may please yourself. But ask before you come."

"Yes, Sir."

J could barely stand. Lewis worked her body until her muscles failed.

Mahogany moaned behind him. "Sir.. may I?"

"No."

She whimpered louder, fingers soaked, back arched.

He waited until her need broke her silence again.

"Sir.. please.."

"Now."

Mahogany cried out, collapsing in orgasm. Lewis turned back to J, untying her slowly.

"Let's go somewhere more private," he said.

J smiled. "I have just the place."

Back at her home.

Lewis stepped inside, eyes trailing across the sleek 4,500-square-foot estate.

"Where's your playroom?" He asked, voice low and sure.

She smiled slowly. "Follow me."

Through a hidden door at the end of the hall, she led him into her sanctuary.

1,000 square feet dedicated to desire.

Saint Andrew's Cross. Wooden spanking horse. A chained web. A black swing. A Sybian.

Even a gleaming stainless steel gyno chair.

And lining the walls: whips, paddles, restraints, masks, and clamps — all pristine.

Lewis turned to her, stripped her bare, and didn't ask.

He bent her over the spanking horse, thrusting into her until she screamed. He tied her to the web, drove into her slowly while whispering filth in her ear.

Then — when her legs trembled and she was out of words — he brought her to the Sybian.

"Straddle it," he said.

She obeyed.

23

He turned it on.

Her breath caught. Her eyes widened. Her thighs shook.

He stood in front of her, pulled himself free, and stroked slowly.

"Mouth."

She moaned, took him in deep — vibrating from below, choking on pleasure.

He held her by the shoulders, hips bucking against the machine, moans muffled by his cock.

He came in her mouth, and she swallowed every drop. Still vibrating. Still shaking.

And he whispered:

"Take it all, J. Lose yourself." And she did.

Mistress J — feared, worshipped, untouchable — shattered in his arms.

Wrecked. Wild. Utterly his.

Grip the Sheets

Inspired by the MCXI Candle —Grip the sheets (Fresh Linen & Lavender).
Every other Sunday, like clockwork, she went to the laundromat.
Not because she needed to.
She had her own washer and dryer. But nothing compared to being immersed in the fragrance of fresh linen and the humming of multiple dryers.
It didn't just comfort her. It aroused her.

Her thighs would press together as the scent filled her lungs. She'd pretend to scroll on her phone while secretly wetting her panties, eyes fluttering shut when the dryer buzzed.

Every other Sunday, she brought her sheets.
It was her kink. Her secret. Her ritual.

Then came him.

She noticed him folding—bald head, well-groomed beard, muscular arms tensing beneath a fitted black V-neck. Tattoos coiled around his forearms like smoke. Her lip found its way between her teeth before she even realized.

He looked up. Caught her staring.
Smiled and said. "Hi."

She walked past and then turned.

"Excuse me, sir... do you always look this good doing laundry?"

He chuckled, rubbing the back of his neck. "I'm not sure, honestly. Maybe today's a special day."

"It is now." She handed him her number. "In case you ever need help folding... or company."

Two weeks later. Sunday night. His place.

He opened the door wearing sweatpants and that same V-neck, even tighter than before.
Defined arms. Broad chest. Her mouth watered.

"I lit something for you," he said, stepping aside.

And there it was—in a square glass jar by the bed.
Lavender. Fresh linen. Flickering low.
Her knees nearly gave out.

"Show me your room," she said.

She shoved him backward onto the bed, straddled him. "Lie back."

He lay back, eyes locked on hers.

She pulled her panties to the side, placed him inside her—wet and tight—and moved her waist like a slow spin cycle. His hands gripped her ass, spreading her open as she began to ride him harder.

She leaned forward, whispering, "I'm going to come all over your dick."

26

He grabbed her by the throat.

"Don't come until I say."

She gasped. Her thighs trembled. A tear escaped her eye.

He began fucking her back—fast and deep.
She started to squirt.

He released her neck just as she collapsed onto his chest, gripping the sheets above his shoulders—shaking and coming uncontrollably.

Afterwards she traced a tattoo on his chest, smirking. "Every other Sunday," she whispered. "That's all you get."

He smiled. "Guess I'll start washing my sheets more often."

Klymaxxx

Inspired by the MCXI Candle — Klymaxxx (Sea salt, jasmine, violet, cedar).

She was 35. Recently divorced.
He was 22. Mature. Observant. Distracted.

They met at a pool hall.
He was with his cousin, but couldn't stop looking at her.

After a missed shot, he walked over.

"Wanna play?"

"I'm waiting for my ride," she replied.

"How about we move to a table, chat before your ride arrives....maybe, you'll allow me to take you home instead."

She laughed. "You're bold."

They talked.

She admitted she was newly single, recently divorced. He listened. She told him she's not looking for anything serious; she just wants to live life, and she felt like marriage was like doing time, not in prison, but some other institution controlled by others' expectations.

Her phone rang; she answered it and said, "Never mind, but thank you." She hung up the phone and said, "You can take me home." He did.

They had a couple more drinks and watched American
Horror Story. He fell asleep on her couch. Woke up the
next morning to the smell of breakfast; he had a
blanket over him.
She was in the kitchen, cooking, in boy shorts and a
tank top.

Plating breakfast like she was hosting a fancy brunch.
Avocado slices. Eggs like clouds. Buttered waffles
arranged in a fan.

"You always cook like this?"

"Only for guests who moan in their sleep."

They both laughed. "That's messed up," he replied.

She invited him back over that evening. "I promise, my
dinner presentation blows breakfast out of the water."

And she wasn't lying.

They ate dinner.
Talked.
Laughed.

But once dessert was done, she pulled him to the couch,
laid her head in his lap, and whispered:

"I've been thinking about you all day."

His erection pressed against her cheek.
She reached in, pulled him free, and took him in her
mouth.

Then she stood, bent over the couch, and said:
"Come thank me for dinner."

29

He did exactly that, he fucked her slowly at first—then deeper.
She moaned, cried, came hard. He carried her to bed, opened her legs in a scissor hold, and unlocked something inside her.

She sobbed.
She squirted.

She collapsed.

"That was my first real orgasm," she whispered.

One year later.

She cooked for him often like they were married.
She tried to spoil him with material things to keep him close.
She got jealous when he didn't text back fast enough.
The more he satisfied her the more her mental state declined.

He knew he had to end it and he did, but he too was addicted to her- to her cooking and her sex.

Her last message:

"I wish I'd never known what it felt like to be with you. You unlocked something in me... and now it won't go back to sleep. I hate you for that. I really do."

He stared at the screen.
Typed a reply.
Deleted it.

Some goodbyes are loud.
Others just... echo.

Ménage

Inspired by the MCXI Candle -Mènage (Vanilla, Lavender & Sandalwood).

They watched him from the window every Saturday.

Rachel leaned on the sill, robe open just enough to show the curve of her ass-round, high, damn near defiant. She was slim, fit, and moved like she had music playing in her hips. Her tattoos peeked from under her robe, teasing what was underneath.

Simone, behind her, leaned against the doorway. Built like sin. Thick thighs. Heavy hips. Tits that made men and women stare too long in Whole Foods. Her body gave soft but powerful. Like she could crush you or cradle you, and you'd beg for both.

"He's early," Rachel said, licking her lips. "8:38."

Simone looked down at him through the blinds. "Still fine."

They'd been watching him for six months now. They called him Saturday Snack.

And he knew it.

He'd glanced up. Just a flick of his eyes toward the porch-sometimes a smirk. Once, he even slowed down. Took a swig from his water bottle or tightened his laces, subtle but obvious.

Simone had to cross her legs that day.

The conversation had been casual at first. "Would you ever?" Turned into "Do you think he would?"

Then it escalated. They started sitting on the porch in short shorts.

Bending over a little slower while watering plants.

One morning, Rachel was outside when he jogged by. He looked, said good morning, and smiled.

She stood up and said, "I see you! I need to come running with you one day."

He turned, slowed his pace, and said, "Open invite." She couldn't wait to tell Simone.

Later that night, things were hot and heavy. Simone pushed Rachel face down on the bed and said,

"You liked that, didn't you?"

Rachel moaned, "Maybe."

Strap-on sessions got rougher. Rachel came quicker. Simone got wetter. And the thought of Saturday Snack was always there, right under the surface.

The next Saturday came quicker than expected.

Rachel had barely tied her robe when she heard the faint rhythm of sneakers hitting pavement.

"8:36," Simone called from the kitchen. "He's early again."

Rachel was already by the door, coffee in hand, robe sliding off one shoulder, ass practically bouncing with every step.

She didn't even pretend to water the plants this time.

Instead, she stood at the door-open just a few inches-arms folded under her chest, lip caught between her teeth.

He jogged up the street, shirtless today. Sweat glistened off his chest like sunlight on caramel. Abs for days. Veins in all the right places.

He saw her.

Slowed down.

Stopped.

"Good morning," he said, breath steady, eyes drinking her in.

Rachel smiled.

"You always run this way?"

"Only on Saturdays," he replied, wiping his forehead with the back of his hand.

She asked if he'd like to come in for a second, take a breather, and maybe have a drink. "We've got top-of-the-line bottled water.. and a few other things that are less healthy but way more fun."

Simone was already standing in the doorway when Rachel brought him in. She was wrapped in a fitted silk robe that hugged every sinful curve. Her eyes scanned Marcus slowly, deliberately, like she was shopping.

Rachel looked back at her and grinned. "Simone, this is Marcus."

33

Marcus nodded. "Pleasure."

Simone stepped forward, hand extended. "I bet it will be." The tension in the room thickened like steam.

They led him to the kitchen, poured coffee from a machine that looked like it belonged in a high-end coffee shop, and handed him one of their expensive bottled waters. They talked casually, but the way they sat, the way their robes shifted with every movement, it wasn't casual at all.

When Rachel crossed her legs, her robe opened just enough for Marcus to see the curve of her thigh. When Simone bent forward to pour more cream, her robe fell loose at the top, no bra. He cleared his throat. "So, uh.. what do you two do?"

Rachel smiled. "We entertain."

Simone added, "We like to host. Interesting people."

Marcus looked between them. "You do this often?"

Simone smirked. "No, however. We were just discussing how we'd like to find something exciting to do- and you appear to be fun."

Rachel grinned and added, "Girl, we're scaring this man off."

Marcus laughed. "So, are you two..?"

Simone leaned back and smiled. "Yes. She's my bitch."

They all laughed. Marcus glanced at his phone. "I should probably get going." They exchanged numbers.

As he reached the door, Simone called out, "You do night runs?"

He looked back with a grin. "Only if I know what I'm running to."

Two days later, his phone lit up with a new group chat.

Simone: We were serious about what we said. We're lovers. But we want to include you.

Rachel: No pressure. No strings. Just pleasure. You in?

Marcus: I'm open. We can hang out and see what happens.

That night, Marcus arrived at their home. Candlelight flickered in every corner-MCXI Ménage melting slowly in the center of the living room.

Simone and Rachel greeted him in robes, barely tied. Music pulsed low from the speakers.

Without a word, they began making love in front of him.

Rachel kissed down Simone's chest. Simone moaned, fingers tangled in Rachel's hair. Marcus sat in the accent chair, hard as stone, watching. They put on a show just for him. Slow. Wet. Intimate.

Then Rachel looked back. "You ready?"

He stood, dropping his clothes as he approached.

35

They pulled him in-literally. One knelt and sucked his balls while the other stroked and sucked his shaft.

He moaned, hips twitching.

Then Rachel climbed on top, straddling his dick, taking him in slow, inch by inch.

Simone walked around the couch, climbed onto the cushions, and lowered herself onto his face.

Their moans overlapped.

Rachel rode him while holding Simone's hips steady. Simone rocked against his tongue while leaning down to kiss Rachel.

Two women. One man. All fire.

And it had only just begun.

Both women came at the same time-trembling, moaning into each other's mouths. They climbed off of him, breathless, and shifted into a messy, passionate 69 on the floor. Rachel on top, Simone beneath her, tongues, and thighs slick with lust.

Marcus watched, stroking himself slowly, until Rachel's thick ass lifted into the air.

He moved behind her and slid in deep, gripping her hips as she moaned into Simone's folds.

"I'm about to come," he growled.

Simone pulled his dick out of Rachel and slid it into her mouth-teasing the mix of both their juices as she sucked him clean.

She swallowed every drop, licked her lips, and smiled.

They collapsed together in a tangled, sweaty heap on the rug-laughter, kisses, and the scent of vanilla, lavender, and sandalwood swirling in the air.

Ménage wasn't just a name.

It was a vibe.

Long Kiss Goodnight

Inspired by the MCXI Candle —Long Kiss Goodnight
(Lavender, Eucalyptus, Almond & Honey Milk).

It was supposed to be just dinner.

Catch up. Laugh. Reminisce about childhood. Maybe a
hug goodnight.

But now he stood at her door, lingering.

The rain had stopped hours ago, but everything inside
her still trembled like thunder was rolling through her
chest.

He looked down at her, jaw tense. Hands in his pockets
like he didn't trust them around her. Not tonight. Not
when she smelled like lavender and honey milk, and
wore that soft robe she always used to curl up in during
college movie nights.

"I should go," he said quietly.

"You don't want to," she replied, just as soft.

His eyes met hers. Something deep passed between
them—unspoken but loud.

She stepped forward, fingers brushing the hem of his
shirt. "It's been ten years. Just.. kiss me. One time."

He didn't answer.

He just leaned down.

Their lips touched—once, like punctuation. Then again, slower. Then deeper.

She melted into him, his arms wrapping around her back like he was afraid she might vanish if he let go. He kissed her like it was the last time—and the first. Like he'd been waiting forever and didn't care if forever ended tonight.

Her back hit the wall.

Still kissing. One hand behind her neck. The other slid down her waist, gripping a fistful of robe and pulling her closer. She gasped into his mouth.

"You always smelled like this," he whispered, breath hot. "Like calm and sin."

She exhaled a shaky laugh. "You're not supposed to say that."

He pulled her bottom lip between his teeth. "I'm not supposed to do this either." Then he lifted her.

Her legs wrapped around him instinctively. She wasn't small—but he held her like she weighed nothing.

They didn't rush.

He kissed her neck. Her collarbone. He whispered things she used to dream about hearing—words full of craving and reverence.

"I missed the way your skin tastes."

"I never forgot how soft you are."

"I want to remember what you sound like when you fall apart."

She trembled in his arms. Let herself fall open to him—emotionally before physically.

He sat her on the edge of the couch, knelt in front of her like worship.

Parted her thighs with gentle hands. Kissed his way up from her knees, slow and patient.

She let her head fall back, robe slipping off her shoulders, breath catching as his mouth reached her center.

He took his time. Tongue slow. Intentional. Listening to her breathing. Adjusting to every moan, every twitch. She gripped his hair. Whispered his name like a prayer. Came shaking—legs clenched around his head.

When he kissed her again, she tasted herself on his lips.

He laid her down, pressed his forehead to hers.

"I want to feel you," he whispered. "Let me in."

She nodded.

When he slid inside her, it wasn't fast. It wasn't frantic.

It was slow. Deep. His hand behind her head. His lips on her neck. Her legs locked around his waist, heels pressed to his back.

Each thrust was a promise. Each kiss was a memory sealed in heat.

She cried.

40

Not from pain. Not from sadness.

From the relief of finally being touched by someone who saw her. Remembered her. Held her like she was precious.

They came together—holding eye contact, trembling, her name, and his breath tangled in the candlelit silence.

They lay tangled on the couch afterward. No words.

Just her head on his chest. His hand stroking her hair. The scent of lavender, eucalyptus, almond, and honey milk curling in the warm air around them.

When she finally spoke, it was barely a whisper.

"Don't leave."

He kissed the top of her head.

"I never should've."

Held her like a man who'd searched a lifetime for the right arms to fall into.

Then he whispered—quiet and raw:

"If you'll have me... I'm yours."

Thirst Trap

Inspired by the MCXI Candle- Thirst Trap (Cherry blossom and grapefruit)

 Two years of teasing across time zones.

It started with a selfie.

He was shirtless, towel slung low, abs glistening like Texas heat. She replied with a mirror pic—tank top pulled up just enough to show the curve of under-boob and the ink that snaked up her ribs. From there, it escalated.

She lived in Philly. He was in Dallas. But their DMs? Lit like a motel neon sign.

They never met. Not once. But every week for two years, they fed each other fire.

She sent thirst traps in silk robes and lip gloss. Sometimes with a vibrator between her thighs, her toes curling in slow motion.

He answered with deep strokes on camera, low grunts that made her tremble. She knew the rhythm of his stroke like her own heartbeat.

They didn't just send content.

They mastered it.

Angles. Lighting. Timing. Every shot was a seduction. A warning. A promise.

Then one night, she broke the rules.

She sent a video—no lingerie, no filter. Just her riding her pillow, moaning his name. Raw. Wet. Real.

He didn't respond for ten minutes.

Then a video came through.

His voice deep and ragged: "You did that to me."

His hand was soaked. His thighs flexed. He was pulsing, trembling, undone.

She clutched the phone with both hands.

Two years. No titles. No plans. Just obsession.

And every night, they went to sleep knowing:

If they ever saw each other in real life.

It wouldn't just be fucking.

It would be destruction.

Wet Rose

Inspired by the MCXI Candle – Wet Rose (Red Rose & Rainwater).

The divorce papers sat quietly on the kitchen counter—unsigned but understood. Claire hadn't touched them in days. She'd walked past them, around them, through them—until they stopped being papers and started becoming a silence that echoed through every room.

Outside, her rose garden bloomed like it didn't care what she was going through. Rain clung to the petals, soaking the earth. She watched through the kitchen window as the landscaper moved between the rows—steady, methodical, unbothered by the storm.

He was younger. Early twenties. Gentle. Quiet. The kind of man who said little, but always listened. Who trimmed her bushes like they mattered. Who never looked at her too long, but never looked away too fast either.

When he finished, he knocked softly and stepped inside.

Claire turned, wine glass in hand. "Didn't expect you to come in the rain."

He shrugged, rainwater dripping from his hoodie. "Didn't feel like staying in."

She moved toward the kitchen island, reaching into her purse. "Do you want cash or prefer Zelle?"

His eyes flicked—brief but telling—toward the stack of divorce papers on the counter beside her.

"This one's on me," he said quietly.

She followed his gaze.

"I should've put those away," she murmured.

"I didn't mean to look."

"I know," she said, voice barely above a breath. "It's okay."

As she reached to set her glass down, a few drops spilled onto the counter. She grabbed a napkin, but before she could wipe it, he stepped closer, reaching for something on her shoulder.

"There's a spider," he said gently.

He brushed it off with a touch so soft it made her skin tingle.

She stilled.

His fingers lingered.

She turned toward him. Slowly. Breath shaky.

"I haven't been touched in a long time," she whispered.

45

He didn't answer.

Just looked at her—steady and quiet—before gently removing the glass from her hand.

And then he kissed her.

The first kiss was careful. The second—curious.

By the third, she was gasping.

His hands found her waist as he guided her backward until her hips bumped the edge of the counter.

That counter.

Where the divorce papers had sat like anchors.

He lifted her onto it without a word. The rain tapped against the windows like a rhythm, slow and steady.

Her robe parted.

He sank to his knees.

And then—he worshipped.

His mouth, warm and wet, moved with purpose. Like he wasn't just trying to make her come—but to unmake her.

His tongue traced her like a prayer.

His lips sealed around her like a confession.

46

When she came, it wasn't quiet.

It tore out of her in a cry so raw she startled herself.
Her thighs trembled. Her fingers dug into the counter.
Her back arched.

She felt everything leave her—the past, the weight, the
years of being untouched and unseen.

All of it washed away under the firm, wet rhythm of his
tongue and the pressure of his lips.

It wasn't just pleasure.

It was release.

It was resurrection.

She collapsed back, breathless, legs still shaking,
staring at the ceiling like she'd just escaped gravity.

He stood slowly, kissed the inside of her knee, then her
shoulder, then her mouth—letting her taste herself and
the storm still clinging to his skin.

They didn't rush the rest.

They moved to the floor. Took their time.

He held her like something sacred.

Fucked her with the same precision he used to
maintain her garden.

47

Measured. Intentional. Focused.

When it was over, she curled into him beneath a soft throw blanket. The scent of Wet Rose lingered in the air—lush, clean, undone.

She rested her head on his chest and whispered, "I don't even know your middle name."

He let out a low chuckle. "That doesn't matter... I don't have one."

They both laughed—really laughed—for the first time that day.

And as the candle flickered beside them and the rain softened outside, she realized...

For the first time in years...

She didn't feel broken.
She bloomed.

ACKNOWLEDGMENTS

To the bold, the curious, and the ones who read between the lines—

This collection wouldn't exist without you.

To those who have supported MCXI Candles in any way—

by spreading the word, sharing a post, or purchasing a candle,

lighting a flame and letting your imagination drift—

Thank you for trusting MCXI to set the mood.

To those who inspired these stories (you know who you are)

Your honesty, chemistry, and wild confessions lit the fuse.

To my tribe—my day-ones, my ride-or-die, and my soft landing (#HS),

Your encouragement gave me the confidence to be unapologetically me.

And to the real ones who understand that intimacy is power—

This book is for you.

— **Eda Boss**

More from MCXI
To experience the candles that
inspired these stories, visit:
www.mcxicandles.com

Follow us on Instagram:
@mcxi_candles

Let the mood linger long after
the final page.